MISTRESS OF
HER OWN GAME

Tales of the Ravensdaughter
- Adventure Five

Erin Hunt Rado

For my beloved Paul

A rare thing is a Walker,
So, gods below: Take care!
Groom them and protect them.
Do not let them despair.

For when a Walker rises,
Realme glory in their eyes,
Mortalia will breathe softly
As Walkers touch the skies.

- from the Scrolls of Imari

Alerice had heard of mead halls, high-vaulted chambers with roughly-hewn beams supporting the wide roofs, and roughly-hewn columns supporting the beams. Two great tables stretched along the hall's sides while roaring pits blazed in the central troughs.

Alerice knew that remote clans constructed such halls as village centerpieces. She had heard of rowdy feasts, and roasting beasts, and flowing tankards. However, she never expected that she would find a mead hall in the Evherealme.

This hall belonged to the Hammer Clan, so called firstly because they bore war hammers, each unique to the warrior who wielded it. So called secondly because they were folk as hard as hammers, both in manner and appearance. Their men broad-shouldered and bearded, their women buxom and braided, Alerice thought their tales were myths conjured by boastful travelers to solicit free drinks. Now, as she supped with the clan's most noteworthy spirits, she could see the substance behind the fables.

Of course, Alerice did not actually sup. She was mortal, and the Realme held no nourishment for her. The roasting joints and foaming brew bolstered the many souls in attendance – and indeed there were many, for the Hammer Clan took pride in offering hospitality.

Alerice sat with the clan elder, Aric. Apparently, he had been quite eager to meet her, not merely because her fame was spreading as the Realme's new Walker, but rather because men of his clan were commonly named Alerick and he wanted to know how her parents had decided upon her name.

Alerice had not been able to answer him, for her parents had never discussed the matter. Nor had Uncle Judd or Grammy Linden, and so any possible connection to the Hammer Clan, no matter how remote, was a historic mystery.

Even so, this small detail did not stop Aric from proclaiming that Alerice was a descendant. The moment he had seen her in armor, with her blonde hair and black scale mail, he had declared that she must somehow be related. Never mind that he was twice her girth and could heft her slim frame single-handedly. He vowed that she was a clanswoman through and through, though Alerice suspected that Aric simply wanted bragging rights.

In truth, she did not mind the manner in which the clan folk pulled her to one side, pushed her to the other, and then slapped her back so hard that she doubled forward. They all meant well. They were a solid people, as roughly-hewn in life as the columns and beams supporting the roof.

Three spits turned of their own accord in the hall's central trough. Coals cooked the meat while movable flat stones regulated the heat. Alerice watched several warriors of varying clans walk to the spits and hack off juicy slices. She noted members of the Wyld, the ashen-and-black painted mercenaries she had met while ridding the traveler's rest of Belmaine, Goddess of Passion and Chaos. They were as noisy and jovial in death as they had been in life, and Alerice smiled to herself, for their queen, T'kyza, would be happy to know of their contentedness.

Alerice also noticed a new clan that called themselves the Painted Women. These were all fearsome females, most of whom had painted themselves indigo and purple. Some had skin the color of rich, brown soil. Some had skin somewhat copperish. All either wore their hair cropped in rows or had no hair at all. Indeed, those who sported bald heads made quite a show of decorating their scalps with white-and-yellow dots that accented their indigo and purple.

Alerice could see from their bodies that each Painted Woman was likely skilled in multiple weapons. She had no idea from which land they hailed, for she had never heard tales of these folk in Navre. Yet how wonderful it was to meet them in this congenial setting.

Alerice glanced at Kreston, who sat two bodies down from her. He pretended to drink as she did, sipping semi-visible brew from semi-tangible tankards. Two Hammer clansmen heartily slapped his shoulders, forcing him to nearly strike his chin against his cup. Then they moved off in the direction of what Alerice considered to be the hall's most striking accoutrement.

This was the great ever-flowing cauldron that floated at the hall's head. To Alerice, it seemed made of solid gold. It had twelve sides, each displaying a clansman's or woman's face amid woven geometric knots. Each knot was dotted with gemstones that winked as they caught the light.

No matter how many guests dipped their mugs, the cauldron never ran dry. Alerice suspected that, as Oddwyn had once stated, these wonders of the Evherealme existed due to the collective consciousness of the mortals whose spirits now inhabited it. The Realme was born of the imagination of the living, men and women, seekers and believers, dreamers and lovers. Indeed, the richness of legends long told had created the splendor inherent within the Realme's very soul.

***

"She called upon Sukaar, Oddwyn," the Raven Queen said as she watched Alerice from her Twilight Grotto. The great tree trunks rooted to the grotto's base gave way to lower and upper branches that stretched toward one another to form six living windows. Less consequential scenes of the Evherealme appeared in five, but the queen's prime pane displayed Alerice in the Hammer Clan's hall.

"She did, indeed, My Queen," the maiden Oddwyn agreed as she beheld the mortal friend whom she had not imagined would have grown so suddenly complicated. Alerice wore the queen's black scale mail. She bore the queen's dagger and crossbow, and yet she had called Sukaar, Father God of Fire, into the Realme so that he could subjugate both the Raven

Queen and the King of Shadows. In so doing, Alerice had transitioned from eager servant to problematic ally.

"Sukaar robbed me of my gem, my Eye," the queen stated, her voice of dark honey belying her misgivings. "All because of my husband's covetous desire."

"Yes, My Queen."

The Raven Queen turned from her pane and fixed her amethyst gaze upon her herald.

"So, what am I to do with her?"

Oddwyn moved a lock of her own white hair sparkling with multi-colored light over her ear. "My Queen?"

"I believe you heard me, Oddwyn."

"Indeed I did, but..." Oddwyn shuffled in the awkward moment of wishing to speak her mind, but not daring to.

"You may tell me your thoughts."

"Great Lady Raven, I am honored. I honestly cannot recall the last time you asked for my opinion."

"Yes, this is true. However, I ask it now. Should I allow Alerice to place herself on display like this? Should I allow her to ingratiate herself with spirits of the Realme, especially to those who were bellicose in life?"

"Hmmm," Oddwyn said, softly rubbing her chin. "A good question, but if I may, I don't think Alerice is ingratiating herself. She is growing accomplished. Word of Sukaar's presence has spread far and wide.

You simply can't keep something like that hidden. And everyone knows that not only did Alerice cause it to happen, she also willingly relinquished the power Sukaar offered her. I have to say that even I was amazed."

The queen pressed her lips into a deep-red line and gracefully turned back to her pane. "Will this not embolden her to look beyond the Realme? When she next returns to Mortalia, she may call upon other gods above. What will she ask of them? How will it affect the Evherealme?"

"I don't believe there's any way to know this, My Queen. I think we can only judge Alerice by what she has done thus far. She chose to remain in your service. She chose to meld with the Realme. That brings her closer to us." The maiden Oddwyn paused, then added, "Do you wish to know what the sorceress Allya told me?"

"Yes, Herald."

"Allya said that as she and Alerice and Kreston prepared to battle the breach of energy you sent them, Alerice was nearly able to create her own portal. Walkers cannot do that."

The Raven Queen neither moved nor responded as she beheld Alerice happily drinking and playing push-pull games with the warrior spirits who dwarfed her.

"Remember how loudly her voice rang out when she called her readiness to us?" Oddwyn continued. "She's unlocking talents that, personally, I did not know she had. It seems to me that the choice is simple. Allow her to leave your service now, and possibly offer Kreston's freedom in the bargain, or nurture her and inspire her and keep her close to you."

"Hmmm," the queen voiced before she lifted her willow-white face. "My husband noted Alerice's pridefulness when he first examined her. What if she grows prideful enough to challenge the Realme?"

"I don't think she will, My Queen. Not unless she feels she's forced to. It's not in her nature. When we all first met Alerice, she stated that she was modest, and I think she has demonstrated this quality several times. She may be prideful, and she's certainly willful, but she is not ambitious. I think she prefers to serve. She just prefers to serve causes that she feels are honest."

The queen said nothing further as she continued to observe her celebrated Walker.

***

"She called upon Sukaar," the King of Shadows complained as he stood within his Hall of Misted Mirrors. Twelve panes of varying sizes and shapes hovered about him, borne upright by smokey tendrils. All were inert, save for his favorite, a pane encrusted with the same crystalline trim that ran along the edges of his long open robe, and topped by the same crystals that formed his crown. "I wonder what our 'honey herald' is saying to the queen about it right now," the king added.

Behind the king floated a specter he had released from the barred pit nearby. This ghost had been a coarse man in life, raw and haggard and suited for ill deeds. Now, he was a mute thing, unable to comment, for he was barely able to comprehend.

The king raised his hand and shocked the spirit, forcing it to contort. The king shocked it a second time, and the spirit shrank in agony. Then the king bade it to regain its composure and stand ready. He would require it, and others like it, in the coming moments. Fortunately, given the manner in which he had briefly wielded his wife's gem, the Queen's Eye, his barred pit of souls was stocked to bursting.

The king focused his pane on the mead hall. The girl was jesting, and walloping, and clanking tankards. And what was his own champion doing? Sitting hemmed in by clansman looking cowed and foolish. Kreston Dühalde spoke little. He made little eye contact. He was allowing himself to be passed over when he should be standing up and outshining that doe-ish blonde child.

"This is humiliating," the king said. "He's languishing when he was once feared. He was such an excellent slayer. Once I brought him to heel, he strode the Realme even as he strode the battlefield. Spirits fled from him here just as mortals did above. But place a girl in his path, and he's ruined. No soul will fear him after this gathering. No soul has feared him since my wife locked his mind away."

The king turned to the spirit and was about to shock it until it ruptured, but instead he chose to banish the bars from the pit and bring forth the strongest spirits. They flew out, and he commanded them to retreat behind his mirrors, which they did, obscured by the many smokey tendrils.

The king turned his head back to his prime pane before turning his shoulders to face it.

"I need my captain back the way he was, burning with red-hot war. I need his wits restored. Otherwise, he's useless." The king shifted his mirror back to Alerice, even as his dark gray eyes came alive with a gambit.

"She wants to be the Raven Queen's Walker? Then perhaps she should learn what that truly entails."

The king turned back to his hall's interior, and with a summoning wave, he commanded all souls to appear before him. Extending both hands, he jarred and shocked them until they began to contort. The souls wailed their misery, but then they roared with vitality as the king transformed them into clawed shadow beasts. Some bore fangs, wings, and human torsos. Some bore human torsos with elongated arms and animal hindquarters. The winged ones stretched their leathery flaps and screeched as they raised their clawed hands in hungry grasps. The animalistic ones sat upon their haunches while resting their great hands flat before them.

The king gestured to the mirror adjacent to his prime pane and conjured the sight of an abbey situated within a verdant vale surrounded by boulder-studded hills. He conjured a portal of black, midnight blue, and deep teal to open along the mirror's surface. Then, with a few quick waves, he commanded his shadow beasts evaporate in smokey wisps, which he thrust into the portal.

∗∗

One of the Painted Women, Pa'oula, who sported purple spirals upon her brown skin, and one of the Hammer clanswomen, Frayla, who wore her hair in long red braids, grabbed Alerice's arms and yanked her from her seat. Aric and his nearby clansmen shouted happily, and pounded the table as the two dragged Alerice toward the great ever-flowing cauldron.

Kreston looked up from his mug, concern for Alerice's well-being clearly on his face, but the clansman beside him knowingly threw an elbow into his ribs, causing him to lose hold of his drink. Kreston glanced at the clansman, annoyed, but then focused on Alerice.

Half the gathering began to chant:
"Drink it down, we all do!
We all know it's Realme Brew!"

One clansman stood to say:
"I'll tell you of a drink that's true!
What's it called?"

The gathering responded with a resounding: "Realme Brew!"

A Painted Woman stood to say:
"With hearty head and golden hue!
What's it called?"

"Realme Brew!" the gathering responded.

A Wyld who looked very much like the mute, Wisp, but who, in the Evherealme, was anything but mute rose to say:
"A drink that makes you rise anew!
What's it called?"

"Realme Brew!" all shouted.

Pa'oula moved Alerice before the cauldron, shoved a mug into her grasp, and gestured for her to dip and fill.

"Go on, give us a line," she said, her copper-brown eyes dancing in the mead hall's firelight.

Alerice wasn't certain what to say, but this was hardly the first time she had been invited to join an improvisational drinking game. She dipped her mug and then held it high. The foam slid down the side of her mug's metal belly. She smiled at it, almost thinking she could smell it. Then she looked at the sea of expectant faces.

"A drink that fills you, through and through,
A drink that's worth a ballyhoo,
A drink I never shall eschew!

What's it called?"

"Realme brew!" all shouted, elongating the last vowel in triumphant conclusion.

"Not bad, Walker!" Aric shouted. "A tad wordy, but not bad!"

His clansmen laughed before they drank.

Alerice glanced at Pa'oula and Frayla, who were gulping down their mugs. Though she knew it was a wholly symbolic gesture, Alerice brought her tankard to her lips, and took a deep draught.

Then she startled. She froze in place, and held the mug before her astonished eyes. She licked her lips, unbelieving because... she could actually taste the drink.

"Oh, come," Frayla said. "You must like it, right?"

"...I do," Alerice said. To check her senses, she drank again. The brew was sweet with a soft alcoholic tang. Its bubbles tickled up through her nose and into her brain. She felt the liquid slide down her throat and instantly warm her stomach.

She had no idea what was happening, for she had been pretending to sip from the several mugs the clan's folk had been placing before her, but this time the brew nourished her.

"Then why do you pause?" Pa'oula asked.

"Because, I can actually taste it."

Pa'oula slapped Alerice on the back, making her double slightly. She tried not to spill her mug as she regained her balance, but Pa'oula paid her no heed as she raised her cup to the gathering.

"You hear that?" she proclaimed. "The Walker can taste the brew!"

Every person in the mead hall roared with pleasure, many rising to toast Alerice while others pounded the long tables and chanted, "Wal-ker, Wal-ker, Wal-ker!"

Alerice made her excuse to Pa'oula and Frayla, and sidled back over to Aric. She resumed her seat next to him, and leaned in for a private aside, which he was happy to indulge.

"What just happened?" she asked.

"You tasted the brew," he said in a fatherly tone. "That means you are becoming one with the Realme, more so than you have ever been. Your spirit and your flesh are taking root here, and you will never be the same."

Alerice stared into his big blue eyes, not certain if this was a natural step for her to make. Could becoming rooted to the Realme portend danger to her mortal self? She had arrived at an unexpected crossroads and taken an inevitable step.

Alerice noticed Kreston staring at her. His expression was one of solemn comprehension, for he could obviously read her concern. His hazel eyes fixed on her, and he leaned in slightly as though he wished to reach out to her. She wanted to pull him aside and ask his counsel, but the sudden sound of disembodied, bloodcurdling screeches rang out in the mead hall, silencing everyone.

"Alerice!" the Raven Queen called, her voice echoing across the hall's towering ceiling.

Alerice saw Kreston recoil, and she quickly stood and raised her mug so that everyone looked at her.

"The Raven Queen!" she shouted in salute.

"The Raven Queen!" the gathering responded.

The air behind the great ever-flowing cauldron began to churn in a spiral of black, midnight blue, and deep teal. Alerice threw a leg over the long table's bench seat and hurried toward the hall's head.

"I'm here, My Queen," she called as she approached the forming portal.

"Alerice," the queen's voice rang out once more. "Hurry to my abbey. Protect my devotees."

Alerice stood before the portal, which did not seem to be opening quickly enough. Through its widening aperture, she could hear more screeches accented by grunts and growls. She heard cries and screams, and she knew that whatever awaited her was a scene of attack, perhaps even a massacre.

Alerice closed her eyes and centered within herself. As when anticipating the fight at the sorceress Allya's lakeside, she focused wholly on the Raven Queen's mark imprinted upon her brow. She felt it pulse, and judged by the comments from the clan's folk that it glowed quite brightly.

She also felt a warm pulse on her jaw along the remnants of Sukaar's fiery scar. She imagined it glowed like embers, as did Allya's great burn, but inured to the mutters about her, Alerice focused all the stronger on opening the portal.

She knew that she affected its expansion, for she felt a shift in its pressure. She raised a hand to the portal, and felt it swirl at her direction. Her other hand floated out to her side and inadvertently touched the rim of the great, golden cauldron.

Alerice felt a shock as she forged an unintended connection between the Realme and Mortalia. However, she had no time to discover what she had created as she opened her eyes to see the interior of a stone abbey on the other end of the wide portal. People ran about in wild panic as strange beasts, some winged and some on all fours, clawed and bit at them.

Alerice drew the Realme crossbow from her belt strap and aimed. The string pulled back of its own accord, and a gleaming black bolt appeared in the flight groove. She fired into the portal, striking one beast about to alight on a woman wearing black velvet robes. Then the bow reloaded as she charged forward.

"Now that's a Walker!" Aric exclaimed as Alerice hurried into battle. His kindred spirits agreed, but then they all regarded the still-seated Kreston.

Kreston saw all eyes on him. He suppressed a shudder at the latent sound of *her* voice echoing in his mind, and then pulled on a military visage as he stood.

Aric looked back at the still-open portal, and then

once more at Kreston.

Kreston followed the Hammer clansman's line of sight, and then arched his shoulders as he stared into the man's eyes.

"It's the queen's business," Kreston stated. "I'm the king's man."

One of the Hammer men smirked, and then offered, "You were the king's man."

Kreston noted the chuckles that the comment solicited. He bit hard on his back teeth, summoning ice into his veins, and for the briefest flash he became what he once had been, that which he now loathed, the Ghost of the Crimson Brigade.

He stared at one accusatory face after another, a snarl crawling onto his lips. Then, he summoned the scratched brand of the King of Shadows to glow upon his brow as he drew his broadsword.

"Damn you all," he said as he turned and charged for the portal.

**

Alerice reached down to grab the woman in the black velvet robes. She yanked her to her feet, and struck a defensive pose before her as she leveled her crossbow and fired at one of the animalistic shadow beasts. The bolt sailed into the creature's heart and impacted with a dark glow that enveloped its body, returned its countenance to a simple spirit, and dissolved it in midair.

"So, that's what these things are," she said as she

sized up the situation.

Alerice stood in a stone abbey where light spilled in from tall windows. She had never seen such a place as this, and though she faced attacking beasts, she could not help but notice the great vaulted ceiling supported by fluted wall columns that split apart into arches. Flat medallions secured each of the arches' juncture points, and the glyphs set into those medallions bore the same mark as the one upon Alerice's brow – a thin oval with a pointed bottom tip capped with a dot, and set on each side with S-curves that fanned out as might a bird's wings.

Resting in the abbey's nave was a two-man-tall statue of the Raven Queen. Its stone bore the same silver veins as the filigree arches in the Evherealme's Convergence. Her likeness was quite true, though Alerice doubted that the sculptors who had crafted it had ever been to the Realme.

But Alerice had no time to admire the craftsmanship, for the abbey was under attack by otherworldly beasts that could turn themselves into smokey wisps and then suddenly reappear in a different location. Recalling how the King of Shadows had sent Vygar and his band of ghoulish thugs to slaughter Lolladoe and the faun clan, Alerice did not hesitate to shoot the beasts as quickly as her crossbow could load.

"You're her, aren't you," the woman commented from Alerice's left.

"Who?" Alerice said as she shot a winged beast in

the chest, dissolving its spirit with the dark glow of the bolt's impact.

"The Great Lady's Walker, her Ravensdaughter."

Alerice gave the woman a moment of her attention. Not only did she wear black velvet robes, she clutched a medallion made of the same silver as the Raven Queen's crown. The glyph cast into it was the same as on Alerice's brow.

This woman must be the abbey's priestess, and Alerice nodded to her as she continued to fire, sparing any devotees from the shadow beasts' fangs.

In the mead hall, souls had gathered near the ever-flowing cauldron, for in touching its golden rim, Alerice had inadvertently joined the cauldron with the portal, allowing the great vessel to retain access to Mortalia and display the abbey battle.

The gathering cheered at each shot Alerice landed, some taking bets as to which shadow beast she would slay next.

Kreston hurried in from the portal. He assessed the plight of mortals fleeing claw and bite, but then he accidentally gazed upon the statue of the Raven Queen. He froze, for the stone bore such a perfect likeness to *her* that he heard the sounds of the hilltop charge where he had lost his lieutenant, Landrew Mülton.

Kreston heard the screams of his brothers in arms whom he had ordered to take a hill that in retrospect could never have been taken. He saw Landrew splayed out upon the field, and was prepared to dive for him and cradle his corpse. If only he had not obeyed the marshal's order to commit the Crimson Brigade to charge that day.

He was about to lose his wits. He was about to go mad. He was going to lose his hold on the moment if he stared at her one heartbeat longer, and so he punched himself across the jaw to break eye contact, and did his utmost not to cower as he lunged for the nearest being, mortal or beast, and began cleaving into it.

Fortunately, he heard only roars and grunts, and he gave thanks to the gods above that his victim has been a beast, not a hapless devotee.

In her Twilight Grotto, the Raven Queen stood stoically as she watched Alerice confront the invasion of one of her most sacred spaces.

Graystone Abbey was a place the Raven Queen held dear. The verdant vale that cradled it rested atop a secret conduit to the Evherealme. She had only to extend her spirit toward Mortalia, and she could touch the thoughts of her devotees. Men and women came to die in the abbey, attended by the Black Mother, as the lady in velvet was known.

The Mother would see to their passing in peace, and assure them that the Raven Queen herself would take their measure and guide them to their places of eternity. To die within Graystone's walls was considered such an honor that towns would pay to transport their most wise and revered. The Black Mother did not acquiesce to admitting the rich and powerful simply for their status, for neither attribute counted among a person's merits or defaults.

Only the wealth of a person's heart mattered, and knowing this the Raven Queen would – upon occasion – appear behind the Black Mother as she tended to a person about to give up their last breath. The queen herself would measure a soul prior to entering the Realme, and in so doing, she had gleaned the spirits required to form her gem, the Queen's Eye.

Now the abbey was in chaos, and the Raven Queen knew well the reason. The King of Shadows had chosen to assault her cherished place. He had chosen to assault her Realme Walker, and everything that Alerice – her champion – represented.

The maiden Oddwyn still stood beside the queen, watching Alerice shoot down more beasts. Then she beheld a struggling Kreston Dühalde, and knew the reason for his anguish.

"He should not be there," Oddwyn said. "As long as he's compromised, he's a distraction."

The Raven Queen did not respond as she watched her Black Mother hurry devotees to the safety of the abbey's private prayer rooms.

In his Hall of Misted Mirrors, the King of Shadows watched the fight from his crystal-topped pane. He discounted the girl, for she would dispatch his shadow beasts in due course.

Rather, his mark was his own man, and Kreston was already in such turmoil that cracking his mind apart would be a simple matter. The king stroked the thin beard that ran along his jaw, and then transformed his face into the Raven Queen's. His crown of dark crystals became hers of bright silver metal, and his dark gray eyes became hers of amethyst.

He turned to one of his inert mirrors and gazed upon himself, causing his torso to haze over with some of the same smokey tendrils that bore up his twelve panes. As they wrapped about him, he saw only his wife's visage, and once he was satisfied with the guise, he turned back to his prime pane and placed his hand upon the surface.

Alerice moved closer to Kreston. As with the demon toad in the river valley before meeting the Wyld, she stood so that they could fight back-to-back. As she had then, she could feel him enjoying the joined combat.

She could sense him becoming himself again, a man who savored a good fight. He seemed happy to guard a comrade's shoulder, while knowing that a comrade likewise guarded his.

Until the Raven Queen's voice rang out from the lifeless statue. "Captain Kreston Dühalde!"

Kreston froze in his tracks, his head snapping toward the statue. Alerice saw the statue's face come alive with the queen's countenance, her amethyst eyes bearing down upon them both.

Kreston screamed and fell to the abbey's cut stone floor just as two shadow beasts attacked from either side, a winged one swooping in to land before Alerice and an animalistic one vaulting forward to attack Kreston.

Alerice only had one shot, and she leveled her crossbow to protect her comrade. Her gleaming black bolt impacted upon the shadow beast mid-vault, and its dark glow dissolved the creature in midair. Then, the winged beast struck Alerice with enough force to send her flying across the abbey and land hard against one of the fluted columns.

In the mead hall, the gathered souls exclaimed a collective, "Whoa!"

Some were about to demand payment of bets, but Aric advanced and *clanged* his hammer against the cauldron. A deep tone rang out, perpetuating as the cauldron reverberated. Knowing this was no longer a gaming matter, but one of life and death, he *clanged* his hammer against the cauldron again to silence it, destroying the latent portal.

He then turned to his kinfolk and guests.

"We will witness this no longer. The gods above will decide their fate."

In her Twilight Grotto, the Raven Queen cast her hand toward Oddwyn, causing the silver scale mail tunic to appear on her torso.

Oddwyn wasted no time in conjuring and

activating her two pixie poles, the blades of which popped out as the queen cast a portal in one of her tree branch-outlined windows. The abbey appeared in a flash of black, midnight blue, and deep teal, and Oddwyn leaped through toward Alerice.

In his Hall of Misted Mirrors, the King of Shadows reclaimed his proper visage and watched for one final moment as the war maiden Oddwyn hurried to his wife's girl of a champion. Then he banished all sights from his mirrors, for he needed to see nothing further.

In the abbey, Oddwyn laid into a few shadow beasts, slaying them with lightning precision. Then she shot for Alerice's side, lifting her into an embrace.

Oddwyn watched Alerice regain consciousness, then wince and reach to the back of her head. Then she saw Alerice's eyes go wide as she looked past Oddwyn's shoulder, and Oddwyn turned to find the same winged beast that had struck Alerice looming large.

From the corner of her eyes, she saw Alerice reach for her Realme dagger and cast it into the beast's heart. Then Alerice stood up from her hold, and though she teetered a bit, she held up her hand so that the dagger reappeared in her palm.

Oddwyn also stood and looked about for any further danger, but the abbey fell silent and secure. Oddwyn nodded to Alerice, but then watched her eyes roll slightly. Oddwyn quickly slung Alerice's arm about her shoulder even as the Black Mother and the Raven Queen's devotees began to advance.

Oddwyn knew this moment would end in a mass of groveling, awestruck mortals if they did not leave immediately. She held Alerice close and moved to one of the abbey's many windows. A portal was already forming, and Oddwyn guided Alerice toward it.

However, as she prepared to leave, she noticed Kreston recovering his wits and standing up.

Oddwyn's ice-blue eyes narrowed, and she mentally ordered, *"Stay away from her, you useless wretch."*

She watched Kreston's shoulders fall and felt his heart sink, but neither mattered as she stepped through the portal with Alerice, heading for the safety of the Realme.

***

"How's your head?" the maiden Oddwyn asked.

"It still hurts, but I'm feeling better," Alerice said as she relaxed against what she would normally describe as a soft mossy rise were she in Mortalia. The 'sky' above swirled in tones of the same deep teal that composed a portal, only currents of lighter blues gave it a daylight hue.

Columns of the Realme's silver-veined stone rose about, each set independently about the mossy rise to form a circle. Black glyphs, the same color as the bolts that loaded into her crossbow, ran down the columns, but what Alerice found the most intriguing were the cascades of silvery glimmers flowing out from the top of each, creating sparkling miniature waterfalls.

The overall area was not vast, and Alerice could see that the 'nothingness' of the Realme surrounded more mossy rises so that the green faded away into the surrounding teal and lighter blues. Fortunately, she did not feel like going anywhere at the moment, though her mind buzzed with questions.

"We don't have healers or doctors down here," Oddwyn said in her gentle voice. "We have their spirits, though, and many have crafted this place of peace over the eons. It's a place for you to recover."

"Thank you," Alerice said, drumming her fingers on her black shirt, for Oddwyn had helped her out of her scale mail tunic so that she could rest more comfortably.

Alerice lolled her head to the side to regard Oddwyn more clearly, then she rolled onto her hip as she prepared to rise. Dizziness struck her, though, and she planted a hand on the moss to steady herself as Oddwyn came closer to help.

"Perhaps you should lie back for a while longer."

"No, I need to sit up," Alerice said, accepting Oddwyn's hand to scoot backward on her buttocks and gain her balance on the rise. She then looked Oddwyn over.

"May I please ask a favor?"

"Of course," Oddwyn replied.

"Please don't take this as any type of a personal comment, but may I please chat with your youthful self? It's not that I don't enjoy you as a Realme sister, but I miss my cousin Jerome right now, and I would find a gentleman's presence a bit more comforting. Plus, you do offer different advice between your male and female sides, and--"

Alerice stopped short, for Oddwyn had already presented his youthful appearance.

"Better?" he asked.

Alerice placed her hand on his and softly said, "Thank you." She drew and released a breath, and then went straight to her point. "Oddwyn, why did the queen call out to Kreston in the abbey?"

"She didn't, Alerice. I was standing next to her the entire time."

"But someone did. Her statue came alive and called, 'Captain Kreston Dühalde'. If the queen didn't do it, who did?"

"I don't know. Perhaps the king?" Oddwyn suggested with a shrug.

Alerice's brow furrowed. "He can assume his wife's guise and invade one of her sacred places?"

"Well, he can present himself anywhere in Mortalia, just as the queen can, and as far as him using her guise, I don't see any reason why he couldn't."

Alerice began to drum her fingers on the moss. "So the king did that to Kreston deliberately. He attacked the abbey, knowing that the queen would send me there, and knowing Kreston was with me in the mead hall. I mean, if the queen knew I was there, the king must have known Kreston was there, right?"

"Probably."

"Then why torture Kreston like that? Is the king angry with him? Or is this how it's always been, which is why Kreston wants so desperately to be free of the king's service?"

"I wish I could help you, Alerice. I truly do, but I have no idea why the King of Shadows does anything."

Alerice continued drumming her fingers as she focused on a column and its sparkling flow. Then she looked into Oddwyn's ice-blue eyes.

"Actually, there is something you can do to help me. I need to know what the queen did to Kreston. I don't wish to confront her about it the way I did about the wizard and the Wyld. I am comfortable serving her, and my soul is becoming more tethered to the Realme. I can feel it, and I don't want any discord with her.

"But I cannot sit by while Kreston suffers, and I'm not going to ask him what happened. I doubt he wants to speak to me right now, and he's probably feeling so lost that if he could end his own life, he would."

"The king won't allow him to do that, and even if he asked someone to kill him, the king would only restore him."

"Well, I heard you call him a useless wretch,

and that wounded him deeply. I saw it." She shook her head and looked toward the brilliant sky. "Oh, Oddwyn. That poor man is utterly devastated, and as much as I care for the Realme, I care for him as well. Please, tell me what happened."

Oddwyn sighed. "Alerice, this is not a nice story."

"Life rarely is," she said. "Life has nice moments, and if a person is lucky, life has more merits than defaults. But I know Kreston's life has been difficult. I just need to know how bad it had to be for the queen to lock up his mind."

Oddwyn blew out through pursed lips before he said, "Kreston Dühalde was captain of the Crimson Brigade of King Kemen of Andelous. He had joined the army when he was ten, and rose through the ranks from runner boy to officer. He was a good leader. He took good care of his men. The Crimson Brigade gained a reputation as a fearsome regiment, and Kemen used that to his advantage. Sometimes, all he had to do was threaten to unleash the Crimsons, and his foes would negotiate rather than go to war."

"But something must have happened," Alerice said. "When Kreston and I were in Basque, the Reef there mentioned that things had gone badly. In Navre, I heard of the Crimson Brigade's ghost, and Allya all but said that the ghost was Kreston."

"Yes, he was," Oddwyn said, "and he'd still be that ghost if he could think straight. That's the reason the Raven Queen scattered his thoughts. Kreston had become a butcher, and one time it went too far.

"You see, the Crimson Brigade was betrayed. Their own marshal ordered Kreston to take a hill on a particularly rough campaign, and then denied him support. The brigade fell, and only a few men survived. Kreston discovered the marshal's plot to undermine the king by sacrificing the men, and he sought the King of Shadows for revenge."

"When you first presented me to the king and queen," Alerice said, "the king offered me the power to defeat any enemy. He must have offered Kreston the same."

"Oh, he did, and Kreston took it," Oddwyn said. "Like you, he didn't know he was a natural-born Walker. You people don't come along all that often, and when the king first saw Kreston, he offered him everything he wanted. Kreston killed the marshal and the rival lords who had put the marshal up to betraying the brigade.

"But then, what was there to do? Kreston had no more enemies, and the King of Shadows hardly wanted a 'champion avenger', which is how the queen sees you. The king wanted souls, and so he started sending Kreston into any type of battle, be it a small skirmish or a full-out charge.

"Kreston needn't have feared dying, for – as I said – the king always had me bring him back to the Realme for restoration. I did it several times. Just as soon as his soul entered the Convergence, the king would protect it while I fetched his body. The king would meld the two, and I would be there when Kreston regained consciousness. He sat where you're sitting now, we talked about what he was doing. He had a conscience back then."

"But over time, that conscience faded?"

"No, it was shattered. In one battle, Kreston found a wounded captain cradling a dead lieutenant, and it triggered the memory of his own lieutenant. He wanted to spare the captain, but the King of Shadows ordered his death. Kreston was forced to obey, and then he went wild. He slaughtered anyone nearby, and then a runner boy attracted his attention. He stalked the child and killed him. Then he murdered the rest of the boys, and after that he attacked the nurses.

"But some of the nurses were devotees of the Raven Queen. Some hailed from Graystone Abbey. They prayed to her, and she came aloft from the Realme to stop Kreston's butchery. Kreston fell to her feet and begged forgiveness. She granted it by affecting his mind so that he could no longer commit wholesale murder."

"That poor man," Alerice breathed as she closed her eyes and lifted her head in thought. She placed one hand on the moss for balance, and allowed the visuals of Oddwyn's story to filter through her mind. Everything about Kreston Dühalde now made perfect sense, and of all the wrongs she had encountered since the night Gotthard had raped her and killed Cousin Jerome, this was the worst she could imagine.

"No wonder he's so desperate for freedom," Alerice said.

"No wonder," Oddwyn said, returning to her maiden form.

Alerice opened her eyes and glanced at her, then nodded and folded her legs as she sat up.

"You must know that I want to help him, Oddwyn."

Oddwyn smirked. "Of course I do. This is *you* we're talking about."

"But this isn't going to be simple. Helping Kreston means I need to outmaneuver the king, and while I've solved many a problem at the Cup and Quill, I've never attempted anything like this before."

"Alerice," Oddwyn said, presenting his youthful self once again. "You really might want to reconsider what you think you can accomplish."

"See?" Alerice said smiling. "I told you that you had different types of advice to offer between your male and female sides. The little colors in your hair even glow differently."

Oddwyn glanced side to side at the bursts of color that naturally appeared in his white hair.

"Be that as it may," he said. "The queen will not allow you to confront the king. I can tell you that for certain."

"Confront how? Am I not allowed to speak with him?"

"No, you are allowed to do that, though she won't

like it, and she'll know that's what you mean to do before you have a chance to ask her permission, which means she'll forbid it before you can bring the topic up."

"Well in that case," Alerice said, climbing to her feet. She felt steady and her wits were sound. Her judgment might be a different matter, but physically she was capable of doing what she fully intended to do. "In that case, you had best take me to the king now."

Oddwyn drew a breath to object as he looked up at her, but she silenced him with a clear, and yet controlled, "Now, please, Oddwyn."

***

Alerice found herself in a field she had seen when standing beside the Raven Queen in her Twilight Grotto. It was covered with small blooms that glowed in rhythmic patterns. Alerice had thought it lovely when gazing upon it through one of the queen's tree branch windows. Now that she was here, the sight of flowers dancing before her, as might birds shifting to and fro in midflight, nearly took her breath away.

Indeed, Alerice would have loved to take her leisure in this wondrous place, were not the King of Shadows standing a few paces off, his back to her.

Oddwyn stood next to Alerice, his posture rigidly formal. He gestured his ice-blue eyes toward the king as if to say, "There he is," and Alerice gleaned that he would have offered a palm in the king's direction if he felt it was appropriate.

Though still quite new to the Evherealme, Alerice found it interesting that Oddwyn was herald to both the king and queen, yet he, and she, clearly preferred the latter over the former. Alerice had declared her preference more boldly, and was proud of it. The king had noted her pride when he had first looked upon her. However, it was a pride that she would never give to him.

Alerice stepped across the blooms, their glows fleeing from her boots as she stepped. She approached the king and reverenced by placing one leg back and lowering her weight slightly upon it while keeping her torso straight. She did not wait to be addressed as she regained her stance, head up and one hand resting on her dagger.

"You should have accepted my sword," the king said, unmoving.

"Your Majesty," Alerice replied.

The king humphed a small laugh. "You wish to speak about Dühalde."

"I do, Your Majesty," Alerice said. "The man who currently bears your sword."

The king seemed to draw and release a breath as he turned to regard Alerice. She studied his calculating dark gray eyes and noted the tension along his jawline. His crown of dark crystals reflected hints of the glowing blooms, as did the crystals adorning his pauldrons and the crystalline trim about his long robe.

"You want me to free him," the king said.

"I want to know what you want of him, Your Majesty," Alerice countered.

"To serve me, girl. What else do you think?"

"But what manner of service, sir?" she asked. "Kreston wishes to be free of you. I don't know if he tried to escape before the Raven Queen took me as her own, but he has certainly tried since. Why do you want to retain someone who hates being tethered to you?"

"Because he's the best at what he does."

"Because he's a born Walker, as I am? Funny that you offered me your blade when you already had someone who knew the shadows."

The king looked Alerice up and down. "You're better. Dühalde is a man of action and experience, but your birth is truer to the Realme. That's why you're becoming part of it. Soon, you'll not be able to leave us, even if you wished to. Soon, you'll be as tethered to it as Dühalde is to me."

Alerice knew this was true, and while it might normally have concerned her, now was not the time to ponder such things.

"I told you to wear your fear openly," the king said, reading her thoughts. "Only then will you master it. It seems you have begun to learn how. My wife's black scales suit you."

"Thank you, Your Majesty," Alerice said, moving her torso slightly aside so that the glowing blooms reflected off her scale mail tunic. Then she leveled a stare and said, "Why do you keep Kreston as a prisoner? He may be the best at what he does, but he no longer wishes to do it. It seems to me that you'd be better served by a mortal who enjoys killing, someone who's a natural butcher rather than someone who's forced to be one."

"A Realme Walker is an asset I do not wish to give up," the king said. "I may be required to force his participation, but he knows better than to resist. He's done so before, and he'll not likely do so again."

Alerice could not help but shake her head. "So he has tried to escape. And still you enslave him. What a cruel thing you are."

"You think my wife is any better?"

"From what I've seen of her, yes."

"Then you have trials ahead of you."

Alerice lifted her chin a bit higher. "Perhaps, but as I told Kreston, the queen released me once rather than argue with me. Then she took me back, and I accepted. And as I said when Sukaar offered me his choice, I wish to remain with the Realme. I have always been a part of it, though I never understood why until I came here.

"But above all, I hate to see people ill-used. Kreston can no longer slaughter in your name. The Raven Queen will not allow it, and I would never do it, so two Walkers are before you and neither are of any use to you."

A moment hung between the Realme's master and its newest servant while the blooms danced as though wind drove their shifting glows.

"And what would happen if I did free him?" the King of Shadows asked. "How would a man like Kreston Dühalde react if he could roam Mortalia again knowing the woman he loved remained in the Realme? Would he pine for you or write poems to you? Would he try to remain at your side? He'd have no blade, and I'd never restore him if he fell in battle. He'd die failed and broken. At least with me he has a sense of purpose."

"You know something, Your Majesty?" Alerice said. "You have a point. He does have purpose while he's with you, but he takes his ease when he's with me. I've seen it in his eyes. For a few moments, he relaxes and becomes the man he longs to be. If it is your desire to enslave him and the queen's desire to cripple him, then it is my desire to comfort him. My father always told me to stand up when I could make a difference, and when I first met the Raven Queen she rightly noted that I was a victim with no advocate. Well, perhaps I will become Kreston's advocate."

"Against me?" the king said.

"Only if necessary, Your Majesty."

The king smiled knowingly. "Girl, you are going to be far too busy to advocate for him. You wish to be my wife's Walker? Then it's time for you to get to work."

Alerice forced a confident look onto her face as the king turned to the field. With a sweeping gesture, he summoned the glow from every flower petal, draining them until they all withered and died.

"Alerice," Oddwyn urged, beckoning her to step away.

Alerice did, even as the king collected and compacted the glows to form the head of a translucent horned sea dragon. The beast was more ghost than corporeal, and Alerice inadvertently stepped backward as the king drew out a great eel's body from its neck. It bore a fish's fanning fins and tail. Long whiskers dangled from its jaws.

The king commanded it to turn in midair and regard Alerice, at which point Oddwyn hurried over to take her by the arm and move her behind him.

The King of Shadows noted the gesture, but paid it no heed as he conjured a spacious portal from the edge of the withered blooms. Within it, Alerice could see a seaside village of hearty, broad-shouldered folk, and she knew that this must be the home of the Hammer Clan.

The king commanded the sea dragon into the portal. It obeyed with a roar. A flicking sweep of its tail caused a whip of air so powerful it nearly hurled Alerice and Oddwyn to their knees. The beast then swam into the portal and dove into the waves with a massive splash. It swam along the surface, its tail churning water to foam, heading for the village's docks and their moored longboats.

The King of Shadows turned to Alerice and offered an "After you" toss of his hand.

Alerice saw the sea dragon rear up at the dockside,

shocking the clan folk and spurring a wave of panic. Anger mounting in her, she placed a hand on Oddwyn's shoulder.

"Herald," she said. "Take us to the mead hall."

***

The Hammer Clan's village was normally a quiet hamlet. Located on an island inlet, its long dock hosted a small fleet. Fishing and trade were the clan's primary activities, for they enjoyed the bounties of the sea at their supper tables, and the metal they forged into magnificent war hammers was found only on their island, and thus was prized.

The clan had heard tales of many monsters that dwelled in the deep, but none had ever expected to see one rising up before them as some semi-transparent demon.

Chaos took hold as folk cleared children from the area while others armed themselves. Men and women ran to the water's edge, while one quick-thinking soul ran to the clan's alarm shield and began clanging out a steady warning.

The horned dragon fell sideways from its rise to cause a massive wave that flooded the dock, washing folk off their feet and sending others leaping into their longboats. A few fell into the sea and scrambled for help amid the wake churned up by the dragon's thrashing tail.

In the mead hall, Alerice appeared to find the

warrior spirits asleep, some lying atop their long tables and others curled up on the floor. Some snored, some belched, and Alerice gave silent thanks that they were not alive, for the smell would have been quite pungent.

She hurried to the hall's head and drew out her pixie pole cylinders as she approached the golden ever-flowing cauldron.

"Oddwyn," she said, looking at the youthful herald who was fixed on her every move. "I'm going to need a portal. A big one."

"Oh-ho-ho, Alerice," Oddwyn gut-chuckled, for a key talent known to every Realme Walker was the ability to guide spirits into combat, and he could see what she meant to do.

Oddwyn hurried to the hall's far side and began transforming the spiritual wall into a churning swirl of black, midnight blue, and deep teal, and he glanced back at Alerice as she raised a single pole.

Alerice struck the cauldron with a tone that resonated clearly. The spirits startled awake, and Alerice struck the cauldron a second time. Brew gushed up over the cauldron's lip and cascaded onto the hall's floor as every spirit shook themselves alert and regarded her.

"Your mortal folk are in danger!" Alerice cried.

She gestured to Oddwyn, who threw open the portal to display the dockside havoc. Aric was the first to stand at the ready and draw the magnificent war hammer from his thick studded belt.

"Kinsmen!" he cried.

"Kinsmen!" his fellow spirits echoed.

"Come on!" Alerice shouted as she sprang over the flowing brew and sprinted for the widening portal.

The horned sea dragon dropped its massive jaw and sank its fangs into the dock, ripping it up from its moorings and consuming a few unfortunate men who could not clear the area in time. Hammer men and women lunged for the beast, doing their best to land a damaging blow. With a few strong head shakes, the dragon cast all aside, impaling some people with massive dock splinters and scattering the rest by forcing them to run for their lives.

The dragon spat out what remained of the dock and roared again, but as it raised its head, a black crossbow bolt lodged in its throat, the dark glow from its impact severely damaging the many floral glows that the king had used to create the dragon's translucent countenance.

It roared again, this time more piteously, but a second bolt lodged in its chest, and the subsequent black glow dissipated its luminous flesh, causing it to half-sink into the sea.

Hammer folk turned to find a blonde warrior in a black scale mail tunic standing on a rocky formation. Behind her the air churned in colors of black, midnight blue, and deep teal, and before the astonished clan's folk could catch a collective breath, the woman gestured to the aperture behind her and shouted, "Onward!"

A roaring rush of ancient voices hollered in response as spirits swarmed out from behind the woman's slim form. She raised her crossbow once more and fired into the horned dragon's eye even as the souls of the clan's mightiest warriors swarmed the beast, laying into it with a volley of unified hammer strikes that *clanged* against its head, back, and ribs.

From her vantage point, Alerice lowered her crossbow, for there would be little action left for her. Unlike protecting the souls of the forest fauns in Uffton, who had been recently slain, daylight had no effect on the souls Alerice had just brought into the living world. The spectral ancestors of the Hammer Clan were long-tethered to the Realme, and feared nothing of Mortalia. True, they would be far more effective at night, but Alerice took pride in their alacrity, and had no doubt that they would soon destroy the king's monster.

Then, the cries of children attracted her attention, and Alerice fixed her crossbow into her belt holder so that she could rush to their aid.

In the field of dead flowers, the King of Shadows watched the scene from his still-active portal. He had compacted its size, but it suffered no loss of clarity. The king nodded despite himself, for the girl was indeed learning what it meant to be a Realme Walker. Her fame would spread all the more quickly once she returned with the Hammer Clan's souls. There was no stopping her in the Realme where he was king, his wife was queen, and she, apparently, was becoming a legend.

"Do you see what she's doing, Dühalde?" the king asked.

He waved his hand, and the veil that had concealed Kreston vanished, allowing him to finally move and speak. He stood, shuddering from the experience of having been locked away while the king had spoken to Alerice. He had witnessed everything while enduring the torture of being unable to intercede. The king smirked at Kreston's anguish, the same way he smirked when shocking a soul to the point of rupture.

"I... I do, My King," Kreston panted, doing his utmost to gain control over himself. His hands were balled into fists. His breathing was quick and shallow. He could not summon ice into his veins, for his body shook with immortal cold, and yet somehow he was able to lock every muscle until he forced himself into near paralysis.

From there, he focused on his breath, inhaling and exhaling with the same cadence that drummers pounded during a funeral procession. Inhale, exhale, until he eventually lifted his hazel eyes to watch Alerice hurry a group of Hammer Clan children away from the water's edge where the horned dragon's thrashing fins threatened to sweep them out to sea.

With one final exhale, Kreston straightened and

leveled his shoulders. Then he paced toward the King of Shadows, his deliberate steps crushing the withered flowers.

"She's doing quite well," the king commented.

Kreston offered no reply.

"I thought for certain that a girl so prideful would assume she needed to battle my creature by herself. Any man would assume that, don't you agree?"

"Yes, My King," Kreston said.

The king regarded Kreston with distaste, no doubt perturbed by his simple replies of "yes" and "no".

"Perhaps that's the difference between mortal women and men," the king said. "Perhaps they don't feel they have as much to prove. Who knows?"

Kreston cleared his throat to chase away the lingering effects of silent confinement. The King of Shadows turned to him and looked him over.

"She's right about you, though. You aren't of any use to me, not while my wife holds the key to unlocking your mind. Perhaps I should seek out a man who enjoys slaughter in my name. You certainly don't, and you can't, and with that girl determined to *comfort* you," he said with a mocking lilt, "you'll only grow more worthless."

Kreston's natural reaction would have been to stand 'eyes forward' so staunchly that he entered his semi-meditative state where he could absorb information without presenting any sign that he was cogent. However, he found a deviant pleasure in watching Alerice manage her battle, mostly because he knew it irked the king.

Kreston smiled despite himself, and then offered his master an unconsciously disobedient smile. As he became more aware of his expression, he allowed himself to wear it openly, for he was striking a blow against his enslaver.

The king's dark-grey eyes narrowed, and daring the dangerous without saying a word, Kreston simply held his head high. He tensed, ready for anything, and stood his ground.

The King of Shadows snarled, and then shouted as he backhanded the air before Kreston so forcefully that Kreston felt the strike land upon his jaw. His head snapped to the side so violently that he thought his spine might snap, and as he tried to regain his balance, he felt a power surge pound his shoulders strongly enough to splay him out onto the dead flowers.

Kreston tried to recover, but the king's power grabbed him by the throat and choked off his air as his master lifted him up and set him on his knees. The king then released his hold, stepped forward, and planted his palm over Kreston's brow.

Searing pain shot through Kreston's skull as he felt the King of Shadows scrape fingernails across his skin. They sunk in as though tearing off a layer of flesh. Kreston clawed at the king's hand, struggling to get free. The pain mounted, but then the King of Shadows shoved Kreston hard, and he fell to his side, panting.

Yet even through the assault, Kreston felt one distinct sensation. The mark that the king had once scratched upon his forehead pulsed one final time, and then ceased. Kreston's eyes snapped open, and he knew that the mark he had once sought – the mark that had proclaimed him as the Walker of the King of Shadows, the mark that had been the symbol of his shame – was gone.

Kreston's eyes went wide. A rush of emotions threatened to undo him, and he fought with every ounce of self-control to keep himself in check. He was free. *He was finally free.*

Kreston planted a boot and forced himself to rise. Then he felt for the implement he had used to take far too many lives, the king's broadsword. It no longer rested at his hip.

Kreston nearly yelped in elation. Instead, he locked his arms to his sides. He longed to insult the king, to lampoon him, to curse him, but he did not dare say a single word. He would celebrate his liberty soon enough. The only initiative that now concerned him was escape.

"Escape?" the King of Shadows commented as he gestured to the still-open portal and the dying dragon. "Why do you think I left the portal open, you fool? You chose the girl over me. Go and take her."

Kreston swallowed hard, knowing he could never trust the King of Shadows. But, he had no other option than to take him at his word. He offered a thin nod and paced toward the portal, noting that he would need to jump into the water and swim for what remained of the dock.

Yet as he approached the portal's rim and the water's edge, the King of Shadows called out.

"Remember, Dühalde. There will be no more restoration after this. You die in Mortalia, you die."

Kreston could not help but smile. "Good," he said, and dove into the waves.

***

"See to your descendants!" Aric ordered his fellow spirits as he pounced upon the sea dragon's sinking head. As what remained of the beast began to lower into the waves, he struck it once, twice, then thrice on the skull, his war hammer sinking further into the creature's luminous outline with each blow. The creature flickered as would a candle spending the last of its wax, and then faded from sight, leaving Aric's soul to hover freely above the water's surface.

Alerice had collected the children and also some teens to her. The teens had not seen the need to seek her protection, but they had gladly approached the blonde warrior wearing black scale mail. Alerice had allowed them to touch and pet it, watching them admire it. She was happy to employ any handy device to keep them nearby until the adults came to claim them.

She did not need to wait long, for now that the

danger had passed, the clan's folk began to collect themselves. Mothers and fathers hurried to her and began to sort through her brood. Smiling, Alerice was happy to greet each of them. She also glanced past them to watch other members of the clan stand in wonder as the spirits she had brought forth gathered on what remained of the dock.

The living folk gathered behind their current chief, who gripped his war hammer and threw his shoulders back as he strode toward Aric. Aric grinned and threw wide his arms, and the two leaders approached, exchanging familial greetings. There was no point in attempting physical contact, which both parties seemed to realize, and as much as Alerice was tempted to offer the two a means to touch, which would entail allowing Aric to possess her body in a Realme meld, the thought of his massive essence in her slim frame made her decidedly uncomfortable.

The last parent claimed the last child, and Alerice smiled before looking out to sea. Then she noticed a man swimming toward her. She watched with curiosity, for he was certainly not a member of the Hammer Clan. Then she noticed the man's familiar build, and her heart leaped.

"Kreston!" Alerice called, a wide smile filling her face.

Kreston waved in mid-stroke, and then dove under the water to make his approach. Alerice watched his submerged form glide beneath the waves, and she moved toward the low footing along the rocky outcrop where he was bound to surface.

He did with a smile, and he offered a happy splash as he treaded water.

"Hey!" she called as he soaked her boots.

"Hey!" he shouted back.

She was about to offer a hand to help him out, but she had seen that mischievous look on her cousins' faces at the brewery. It had always appeared as they planned a prank, and she stood back to regard him.

"You're not going to pull me in with you, are you?"

"Tempting, my dear. So tempting, but no."

"All right, I'll trust you," she said with her hands on her hips. "But don't make me regret it."

There was sincerity in Kreston's eyes as he said, "Alerice, causing you regret is the last thing on my mind."

Alerice smirked with mock suspicion, but knelt on one knee and offered a hand to help him climb onto the rocks. He scrambled out of the water and got to his feet. Then he shook his head and wiped his brow and eyes.

At which point Alerice noticed that the mark of the King of Shadows, the series of slashes he loathed so greatly, no longer appeared on his brow.

"Kreston," she breathed.

He met her gaze.

"I know. He let me go, Alerice. He set me free."

"Oh, Kreston," she half-cried out.

She was about to rush to him, but his clothes

were sopping. She hesitated a moment, and then decided to throw caution to the wind. They both moved toward one another, and he folded her into an embrace, pressing her to him.

She felt him chuckle. She felt his joy. She could not have been more elated for him, and she did not resist when he simply could not contain himself a moment more.

"Alerice!" he cried aloud as he hefted her into his arms and spun about with her. She laughed with delight until she felt him beginning to lose his balance, at which point she wiggled a bit so that he might set her down.

He did, but he beamed so greatly that he stepped to the edge of the rocks, held wide his arms, and let loose with a mighty, "Ho-ya!"

From the corner of her eye, Alerice saw that he attracted a few glances from nearby folk. Fortunately they were so fixed on uniting with their most revered spirits that they paid little heed.

"Ha!" Kreston exclaimed as he turned back to Alerice.

She smiled and nodded. "Good for you, sir."

He let his arms dangle at his sides as he exhaled. "Good for me," he softly agreed. Then his expression became more reserved as he stepped toward her. "I wish I could say good for us."

Alerice drew and released a breath, then took a step back. "I know you do. But take this triumph and enjoy it. You deserve it."

"I don't know that I do. I have a great deal to atone for, but gods above, Alerice. At least I'm not *his* any longer."

"You're not worried that he might reclaim you? Remember what you said to me when the Raven Queen released me? That once the Realme has had you, it can always take you back."

"I did say that, and the queen did take you back. I guess I'll always live with the risk that the king might try to claim me again."

"Try?"

Kreston smirked. "I won't go back without a fight."

"No, I suppose you won't," she said.

Alerice watched Kreston come close. He moved a lock of her blonde hair behind her ear, and then ran his fingertips along the burn scar that Sukaar, Father God of Fire, had left upon her jaw. She knew that he wanted to kiss her, but he held back.

"You don't want to come with me, do you?" he asked.

"Kreston," she said. "It's not you. I don't want to go with anyone. I've never wanted to go with anyone, and I can't tell you how many times I've been asked. You think those men who competed with love poems to win free drinks at the Cup and Quill didn't mean the words they wrote? You think my uncle and aunt and grammy didn't want me to find someone? Even my cousins tried putting their friends forward."

"I understand," he said. "Who wouldn't want to

marry you? You're so easy to love."

He cupped his hand to her cheek, and she cupped hers over his.

"You're a good man, Kreston Dühalde," she said. "And I want you to spend the rest of your life doing good things. Promise me you won't waste this chance."

"What?" he said, his expression suddenly concerned.

She pulled away from his touch.

"I said I don't want you to waste this chance," she repeated.

Kreston patted his palm over his ear, and shook his head. "I can't hear you," he said. He opened and shut his jaw a few times, then shook his head again.

"Kreston," Alerice said, taking hold of his shoulder and forcing him to lock stares with her. "Kreston, look at me. Can you hear what I'm saying?"

His expression conveyed that he could not, and she noted his anxiety as she looked about for help.

"He cannot hear you because I do not wish him to hear me," the Raven Queen said in her voice of dark honey.

Alerice looked up to see her matron standing stoically on the rocky outcrop. Kreston began to look as well, but Alerice pulled him close and forced his head away.

"Cause him to face the sea," the queen ordered.

Alerice maneuvered Kreston about, and guided him to face the waves breaking below their feet. He tensed, for he likely knew what was transpiring, and he lowered himself to his knees and struck a rigid pose.

Alerice placed a hand on his shoulder and gripped his wet tunic before she paced about his side and reverenced.

The Raven Queen floated down to her. She surveyed the clan meeting upon the ruined dock, and her amethyst eyes filled with disapproval.

"Look at what my husband has done," she said. "He assaulted my abbey because he wished to strike at me. He assaulted these people because he wished to strike at you. Alerice Linden, my Ravensdaughter, you will no doubt have qualms with what I am about to say, but I must task you with striking at him."

"But you said you would never openly act against him, My Queen."

"Nor am I," she replied. "But this is a specific task that must be completed now, while he has no champion. This task will prevent him from enslaving anyone else. I now send you to his shrine on the seaside cliffs where you will destroy his gateway and those who guard it."

"Those who guard it?" Alerice repeated. "So, you're sending me to murder people?"

"Alerice, if you could destroy the gateway by some other means, I would accept, but you cannot. You must strike while my husband is compromised. Without his shrine, he will not have a fabled place where men seek him out. Without his gateway, he will not be able to send forth his Shadow Warriors to test the mettle of men who would serve him.

"Let Kreston be his last servant. He does not deserve another, and he certainly does not deserve a Walker. It is the Mother Goddess of Water and Wind, Imari, who has written that all Walkers should be cherished. Look how my husband has mistreated Kreston. Look at how he assails you. You must destroy his shrine, and this time I must command it. Come to your peace with this task, Alerice, but do not challenge me, for I will have you obey."

Alerice pressed her lips together. Then, she found herself asking, "How... do I find it, My Queen?"

"Call to me, and I will deliver you."

The Raven Queen held Alerice in her infinite amethyst gaze. Then she turned and raised a willow-white hand toward Aric and his Hammer Clan souls. Alerice watched the spirit warriors raise their hammers to her, bid farewell to their descendants, and then raise their heads. The queen gestured for them all to come to her, and Alerice saw them dissolve into glittering metallic wisps that flew to the queen as she faded into an opening portal of black, midnight blue, and deep teal.

Alerice exhaled heavily. Kreston responded to the sound of her breath, and quickly rose to face her.

"What did she tell you?"

"Kreston," Alerice noted. "You didn't say *she* the way you normally do."

Kreston paused, realizing this was true. "No, I

didn't. Funny. But what did she say?"

Alerice sighed, turning about as she patted her hand against her thigh. Kreston stepped into her line of sight and pressed his gaze. She met his hazel eyes, and then shook her head.

"She wants me to destroy the king's shrine."

"The cliffside shrine?"

"You know it?"

Kreston looked at her incredulously. "Know it? Of course I know it. Where do you think I sought him out? Where do you think anyone seeks him out?"

"I wouldn't know," Alerice said flatly. "I'm just a tavern maid, remember?"

Kreston grimaced. "Well, you're hardly that any longer. You're a Realme Walker, and from what I can see you're becoming accomplished. The cliffside shrine has existed for ages. It's a fable told to every man in uniform. We've all heard the stories, especially on the nights before a battle when we don't dare keep a fire going for fear of giving up our position. Any man brave enough to seek the black fire and climb the cliffs can light the basin and call upon the King of Shadows. And he will answer, as he did for me."

"That's all? Get some black fire and light a basin?"

"You think it's easy? Monks guard the flame, and they can shadow-step so quickly that you won't be able to see them move. The cliffs are damned tricky to climb, and you can fall onto the rocks below. And then when you get to the top, if you get to the top, and light the basin, the king will send his Shadow Warriors to test you. You can't beat them. No one can beat them, but the king watches the fight, and if he thinks you're good enough, he lets you live."

"Wonderful," she said. "So basically, I have to defeat the monks--"

"Kill the monks."

"What?" Alerice gasped.

"You'll have to kill them, Alerice. There's no way they're going to let you make the climb."

Alerice moaned as she despaired the thought. "So the King of Shadows was right. The queen can be cruel."

"She's not being cruel," he said. "Not in this. Alerice, remember in Basque when you discovered that the inn master was selling children? Remember how he threatened to kill one right in front of you? You didn't hesitate to kill him, did you?"

"I had to save the child. But I didn't kill his wife. I gave her to the Reef. She was hardly innocent, but it wasn't my place to judge her."

"It's not our place to judge anyone we fight," he said. "Do you think I strolled out onto a battlefield and said, 'I think I'll kill someone bad today?' No. I fought because I trusted the judgment of those I served. I resisted the King of Shadows because he betrayed that trust. These monks are not innocent by any means, and the queen is doing a service to future men by having you destroy them."

Alerice sighed again as she mulled the moment

over. "So kill the monks, and fight the Shadow Warriors, and then destroy the shrine? The Raven Queen expects me to do this?"

Kreston paused and then said, "I think she expects *us* to do this."

"Us?"

"Why else would she task you here? She knew we'd have this conversation. She knows we're having it now, and she knows I won't let you do this alone."

"But Kreston, if you fall, you'll die."

"Alerice," he said with a thin smile. "If you think that bothers me, you're wrong."

***

The night's wind slashed Kreston's face. Blowing in hard from the ocean, it whipped his salt-and-pepper hair and froze him to the bone. He longed for a hooded cloak, not that he'd need it for long. He looked up at the crags rising overhead, and heard the roar of the ocean waves below. To the side, he caught a faint trace of the cave where the monks kept the black flame. He was completely insane to be doing this again, but he was not about to allow Alerice to do this alone.

She had left him a moment ago, after Oddwyn had delivered them both via portal. The waning moon bathed the rocks in soft silver, but it would not provide enough light to find all the toeholds. Kreston would need to remember where most of them were, though years had passed since he had made the climb.

He hugged himself for warmth, trying to recall how driven he had been back then. His brigade had just been slaughtered. His lieutenant had just been murdered. He had just discovered the marshal's plot to betray his men and leave them without support as they faced an encroaching enemy on that damned hill. He had sworn revenge, which had consumed him as he sought the King of Shadows.

He had ridden to the seaside trailhead. He had found his way along the narrow path. For nearly two leagues, he had been forced to crawl, leap, and cling.

It was all appropriate, for the quest to reach the king's shrine should be difficult. Only the best men could solicit him, and the narrow path to the monks' cave was merely the first challenge. Those who were faint of heart would have turned back half-way, or better still never have attempted the path in the first place. He had, though, and fortunately this time Alerice had asked Oddwyn to deliver them to the cave mouth. If only she would return so he did not freeze to death.

Kreston felt a shiver chase up his back, one that was not born of cold. He turned about, and though the night concealed the swirling tri-colors of black, midnight blue, and deep teal, he could make out the edges of an opening portal.

Alerice stepped through, her blonde head and fair face seeming to float in the darkness that concealed her black scale mail. Kreston watched her look about to mark her bearings, and then regard the thrashing waves. She shivered as the cold struck her. Kreston advanced to hold her close, but she held up her hands to refuse.

He nodded, for words were useless. They both knew what needed to be done, and Kreston began to turn toward the cave. However, something in the sea caught his eye, which he regarded once, then twice.

The waves were breaking along a centerline, as though flowing to both sides of some great cresting object. He reached for Alerice so that he might maneuver her behind him, but she stood her ground.

Kreston moved abreast of her, and saw the Raven Queen's mark begin to glow. Panic struck him, for he could not bear the sight of the White Lady, as he had once called her. He had no idea what would happen if he beheld her or heard her voice, for unlike earlier at the Hammer Clan's village, he now heard everything.

For Alerice, the sensation was intriguing. She felt her mark pulse, but not in the typical way it did when the queen approached. She glanced at Kreston, who openly wore his worry, and placed her hand upon his forearm. He responded to her touch, and she felt it was safe enough to leave him and move toward the waves.

Kreston did not advance with her as she stepped closer to the edge of the narrow trail, watching with fascination as cream-colored shapes, illuminated by the moonlight, began to dance below the ocean's surface.

They were otherworldly figures. Alerice counted six darting gracefully. One crested the surface, which had gone surprisingly calm, although the waves further away continued to thrash. Alerice felt a breath of cool wind caress her face, replacing the cold slices that had assaulted her.

The figure was exquisitely long-limbed with hair of seafoam green that seemed tossed by ethereal currents.

Alerice could not be certain if it was male or female, for it was nondescript, quite unlike Oddwyn who clearly presented as a youth or a maiden. Another figure crested and then another, filling Alerice with delight, and though she had no idea why the Raven Queen's mark glowed so brightly that even she caught sight of it, she knew that these beings presented no danger.

"Sorgini," Kreston breathed as he approached to stand at her flank.

"Sorgini?" Alerice asked, turning her head slightly to him, for she could not take her gaze off the half-dozen wonders. Now that all had risen, they bent down to flatten the waves as chamber attendants might flatten a carpet runner.

Then, Alerice saw Kreston fall to one knee and bow his head, and she fully regarded him before she looked once more at the ocean.

A breath of warm perfumed air blew in. The scent was so intoxicating that Alerice inhaled deeply, remembering the bowl of scented flower petals she used to keep on her bureau in her room at the Cup and Quill. All traces of the salty air vanished, as did the cold, and Alerice swallowed in anticipation of something wondrous.

"Bow your head, Alerice," Kreston said, his own still low. "The mother goddess approaches."

Alerice swallowed again, her eyes going wide at the suddenly emerged sight of Imari, Mother Goddess of Water and Wind. She fell into her natural reverence, but for some reason she did not bow her head. She fully meant to, but she simply forgot.

Imari's gown was made of the same seafoam as her Sorginis' hair. The Sorgini tended its volume as she floated toward the shore. Imari's hair was light blue and silver, and was tucked into lovely folds adorned by combs of coral and pearls. Her flesh was close to Alerice's own tone, and her meridian-blue eyes sparkled.

Gentle wisps of wind played in her gown's sleeves. Small pools of glistening water formed as her feet touched the rocky path. She commanded the moonlight as though it was meant for her alone, and she bade Alerice to back away as she came forward.

The Sorgini fanned out, three to Imari's sides, and held their thin hands up toward her.

"You may stand and behold me, Captain Dühalde," Imari bade in a dulcet double-voice.

Kreston stood, and yet as he raised his head, Alerice could see tears in his hazel eyes.

"Alerice Linden," Imari beckoned as she reached out to stroke Alerice's blonde head.

Alerice could not help but feel her own tears forming, though she tried to dam their flow.

"A true Walker of the Realme," the goddess continued. "As are you, sweet Kreston."

"For Walkers are true beings, who rightly know their minds. Inspired by the gods, their worth is well defined," the Sorgini chanted.

"Indeed their worth is well defined," Imari said. "So I have observed across the ages, and have set down in my scrolls."

"A rare thing is a Walker, so, gods below: Take care! Groom them and protect them. Do not let them despair," the Sorgini chanted.

"So, gods below, take care," Imari repeated. "I am not certain this has been the case, certainly not with you, sweet Kreston."

Alerice watched Kreston close his eyes and say nothing. He stood at attention as any military man would, only his shoulders were not arched back. He merely forbade himself any response.

"I do not despair, great goddess," Alerice said to focus attention on herself and spare him.

"No, you do not," Imari agreed, her double-voice filling all available space. "And if the Raven Queen cherishes you, as I have decreed, you will become an asset far greater to her than her Eye."

Alerice suddenly suspected the reason for Imari's presence.

"Mother Water Wind, the King of Shadows was jealous of the Queen's Eye. He stole that gem from my matron. Do you believe he wishes to steal me?"

A tiny "Ah" escaped Kreston, and Alerice glanced at him, seeing his anxiety. He likely had not thought of this notion before, and now it spurred dread.

"Not even I can see the king's mind," Imari said in a coo that was as strong as it was calm. "But were he to covet you, I could understand his desire. My husband, Sukaar, desired you," she said, running her fingertip along the burn scar on Alerice's jaw. "Were you a woman of learning and spell craft, I would have welcomed you as my one devotee in generations. But you were born to the shadows, and to the shadows shall you be forever tethered."

"Regard them now, these Walkers, gods above and gods below. The Realme has kissed Mortalia, forever now, and long ago," the Sorgini chanted.

"And now I will add my kiss," Imari said. She bade Alerice come closer, and Alerice stepped forward without fear. Imari brushed the blonde hair from her brow, and kissed her forehead atop the Raven Queen's mark.

Alerice closed her eyes, for a feeling of transcendent peace filled her toe to top. She did not sense all-knowing wisdom. She did not feel a rush of power. She simply knew who she was and who she was born to be, a child of the shadows conceived in that rare set of circumstances when, as Imari's scrolls stated:

The Serpent Father Fire
Loves the Mother Water Wind,
When L'Orku's breath of thunder
'Cross the mighty sky ascends.

And yet Alerice felt as though she might be more than a Walker. She did not know how or why, or what this new feeling might entail, but she accepted it for what it was and where it might guide her.

"First a god, now a goddess. You're making powerful friends," Kreston said.

Alerice did not know what to say. Imari had receded into the ocean, her Sorgini with her, and the egress had been as lovely as the ingress. Alerice noted that they both still had tears in their eyes. She reached to Kreston, but he pulled his head away. She sniffed her own tears back.

"Why do you weep?" she asked.

He swallowed hard.

"Because when I heard her voice, I had a flash of memory. She came to me as well, here in this place, before I made the climb. I remember now. Her Sorgini were with her then too. The moon was waxing, but not far from where it shines now on the waning side. She offered her kiss to me, just as she offered it to you," he said, tracing the mark Imari had left on Alerice's brow, a blue upturned curve that wove through the short pointed oval of the Raven Queen's mark.

"She said that I was a born Walker, and that I

should be cherished, but I've never been cherished. My birth was so long and painful that I crippled my mother for life. My father hated me for it. My siblings followed his lead, along with everyone I knew as a child. I had no idea I was a Walker. How could I? I ran from home. I found comrades in the army. Cherished," he commented derisively.

"But if I had taken Imari's kiss," he said. "If I hadn't been so..."

"Lost?" she offered.

"Proud," he said flatly. "I told her 'no'. I told her I didn't need anyone's kiss. I asked her where her kiss had been when my men were being butchered? Who in the world was I to say something like that to *her*, a goddess?"

Alerice noted that, for the first time since she had known Kreston, his inflection of that particular pronoun conveyed the utmost respect.

"And perhaps if you had told her yes, things would have been different between you and the King of Shadows?" Alerice asked.

Kreston nodded, sighing heavily.

Alerice nodded in response, but as they turned toward the monks' cave, she was well aware, that he was well aware, of how greatly he required the full use of his memory.

***

Alerice insisted on entering the cave before Kreston. He insisted on standing tall at her back.

Neither had drawn a weapon, Alerice because she did not intend to and Kreston because he had none. He also knew that blades would be of no use against devotees who could step so quickly that he could not trace them.

The cave was empty, save for a brazier in which burned black flames. It stood on a cast-scroll metal stand that bore soaked-and-ready torches about its three legs. The cave was considerably warmer than outside, and Alerice wondered if the heavy atmosphere was meant to lull those seeking the King of Shadows into a state of unreadiness.

Kreston said nothing as he squeezed Alerice's shoulder. She stepped forward, only to be met with a series of quick rushes all about.

Kreston squeezed again for her to hold, which she did. The rushes continued about her sides in a frenzied fashion meant to confuse her, and for a moment they did. However, she focused her consciousness on the Raven Queen's mark, and she heard a chorus of howls ring out from the cave's interior.

She watched as the air about the cave seemed to swish as though several ghosted shadows had assembled, and she took one decisively defiant step toward the brazier.

"Be gone from this place, wretched girl," a voice whispered.

"Show yourself, shadow," Alerice replied. "I'll not move, and you must know that I mean to ruin this place."

"To your own ruin," came another whisper.

"Oh, stop," Kreston said. "Enough with the disembodied voices. Neither of us are impressed."

Alerice glanced up over her shoulder. "Well said."

"Thanks."

A whoosh of air assaulted them before five shadow monks appeared opposite the brazier. Their skin was yellowish-gray and their eyes were the same dark gray as the King of Shadows'. They were lean and tall and Alerice noticed that the fabric of their tunics and cuffed pants shimmered dully. Perhaps it had been imbued with dust from the crystals with which the King of Shadows adorned himself.

"Take a torch if you can, wretched girl," one monk offered.

"Ah, that's right," Kreston said. "They can't attack until you try to light one."

"Really," Alerice commented. "So we could stand here and discuss our favorite color, or make jokes, or waste time, and they'd have to stand there and listen?"

Alerice felt another volley of rushes dart past her, only these began to snipe at her face and body, nearly pushing her off balance. The rushes were definitely malevolent, and Alerice thought better of making another jest.

Kreston strode forward and grabbed hold of a torch.

"No, Kreston," Alerice said, but the rushing

intensified.

Kreston grabbed a second torch and attempted to use them as Alerice might use her pixie poles, but the air ripped about him right and left, forward and behind, beating into him and forcing him down to his knees.

Alerice drew her Realme dagger and leaped beside him. She plunged it into the heart of the black flame, tolerating the heat as her blade began to glow. She sensed the rushes assaulting Kreston abate, and she held her blade aloft.

"If I take a torch and you attack," she stated, "this weapon will find you. You all know this. Stand down, warriors of the king, for I do not wish to harm you. However, I will complete the task that my mistress has given me."

"Slay us if you can, wretched girl," a monk said.

"Get them, Alerice," Kreston urged, cradling an arm about his midsection.

Alerice smiled as she closed her eyes and gave her entire being over to the Raven Queen's mark. Again, she heard howls, but they faded as she heard the roar of ocean waves. She felt the power of water and wind fill her soul, and somehow she knew that she should mix this new force Imari had granted her with the love of the Realme and its blessed shadows. She conjured the image of the youthful Oddwyn waiting in the Hammer Clan's mead hall with Pa'oula and six of her Painted Women, all of whom bore short spears.

"Send them to me, Oddwyn," Alerice ordered.

In the mead hall, Oddwyn saw a portal begin to open in the Realme's signature tri-colors of black, midnight blue, and deep teal. His ice-blue eyes fixed on the aperture, and he straightened with surprised respect.

"You're getting good at this, Alerice."

Oddwyn drew his hands apart to widen the portal, and the Painted Women charged forward.

In the cave, the shadow monks all stood still as the Painted Women poured in. Their quick steps were of no use, for they could not elude spiritual eyes. The Painted Women thrust their spear tips, which the monks parried with open palms. The women parried their counter-attacks with their spears' shafts, and then riposted by slamming their spears' butts into the monks' bodies. The attack was quite effective, for the shadow monks had given up part of their mortality to attain their speed, leaving them vulnerable to spiritual assault.

Kreston thrust his two torches into the brazier so that the black flame consumed the tips. Then he withdrew and tossed one to Alerice.

"Come on!" he said as he bolted from the cave.

Alerice sheathed her dagger and called, "Pa'oula!"

The Painted Woman turned to her and grinned. Alerice held wide her arms, and Pa'oula flew toward her, leaping into her flesh in a Realme meld. Alerice steadied her balance and then opened her eyes, which had turned copper-brown.

***

Kreston stood at the base of the crags, his black flame torch burning in lurid licks. He watched Alerice sprint toward him, and was about to caution her how to place the torch in her mouth so that she could make the climb. However, he was gobsmacked to watch her do so without instruction, leap clean over him, and begin to scale the crags.

Achieving a solid hold, Alerice withdrew the torch from her mouth to shout, "Come along, Crimson Ghost."

Kreston knew that Alerice's voice was not her own. He caught the faintest trace of her eyes, and then jammed his torch between his teeth. He leaped up after her, noting that she began to ascend with surprising agility.

Alerice leaped high from her toehold near the top of the cliffs. She landed in a crouch on the upper plateau, but then her head snapped to the side to behold the basin of the King of Shadows. It rested within an open stone shrine, the eight arches of which supported a concave stone cap.

She sprinted to the basin and cast in her torch to ignite the oil-soaked peat, but then she heard a man grunt, and she hurried back for the cliff's edge. Glancing over the side as wind sliced her cheeks, she saw Kreston struggling with his hold.

"Throw it up!" she demanded of his torch.

He hurled it at her. She leaned over the cliff edge as she reached for it, but she leaned too far. Her body teetered, about to fall, when Kreston vaulted himself up and planted his palm against her breast.

He pushed her back, and Alerice regained balance. She reached down to grab hold of his arm, and with strength that seemed too great for her body to bear, she cried out as she hauled him high enough to crest the edge of the plateau.

Then she fell back to her haunches, panting.

"Get out of her!" Kreston shouted as he kicked the back of Alerice's black scales. Alerice saw him reach down and grab his torch, and then he hesitated.

He seemed prepared to kick her back again, but fortunately Pa'oula's spirit flew out of her breast, and Alerice heaved backward.

She began coughing. Kreston reached down and lifted her to her feet, but as Alerice watched him turn toward the basin, she saw the king's two Shadow Warriors standing in his path, swords drawn.

Alerice regarded them, then Kreston, and then she grabbed Kreston's torch to throw it into one of the warrior's helms. It landed within the empty space, causing the specter to shriek and recoil.

"What are you waiting for?" Alerice said as she grabbed the pixie pole cylinders from her belt and activated them so that their bladed poles popped out. She passed one to Kreston and drew her Realme dagger with her free hand.

Kreston bore his pole two-handed and charged.

He laid into both warriors, but neither fought him with much vim. Just as well, for Alerice had already planned a countermeasure.

She moved behind him and tugged the back of his belt. He glanced over his shoulder, and she gestured for him to retreat. She guided him to the edge of the shrine's base, and motioned for him to step off.

"What's your plan?" he asked.

"Get clear, and I'll show you," she replied.

He did, following her lead. The Shadow Warriors reached the shrine's circumference, but did not step down.

Alerice motioned for Kreston to hold his ground, which he did as she again gave herself over to the queen's mark. She felt it pulse. She heard Imari's waves. She felt the Realme, and then she called once more, "Now, Oddwyn!"

In the mead hall, Oddwyn opened a second portal and turned to Aric and his clan. They raised their war hammers, hungry for another opportunity to do battle in Mortalia.

Oddwyn offered a "There you go" gesture, and then quickly jumped back as the broad warriors cried out and charged into the portal.

The sky swirled above the shrine's concave cap. The portal opened, and the Hammer Clan flew down from its center. They launched themselves upon the cap and began pounding the stone. The *cracking* rang out into the night, and Alerice smiled even as she winced, for the attack sent out shockwaves that reverberated inside her ribs.

Kreston led her away toward a grouping of boulders where they could watch the demolition from a safer distance. The incessant pounding fell off into the moonlit night as the Hammer Clan collapsed the cap and began assaulting the columns.

Alerice looked at Kreston, who savored the destruction of his place of enslavement.

"You could always join them," she offered.

"How?" Kreston half-chuckled.

"You're still a Realme Walker, Kreston Dühalde. You could take one of their spirits into your flesh and--"

"Alerice, stop. I've never tried a meld, and I'm not going to start now."

"Fair enough," she said.

Aric and his men began to topple the columns. The Shadow Warriors stood stoically as the first crashed down and broke apart. Aric's men downed the remaining columns, and soon the Hammer Clan began reducing all stone to rubble.

The air over the Shadow Warriors began to shift, and the king's knights dissolved into nothingness, leaving the Hammer Clan happily plying their well-renowned skills.

Kreston handed Alerice's bladed pole back to her and folded his arms across his chest. "Who'd've thought."

"I know," she said. "I actually wasn't certain they would be able to successfully destroy this place, but Oddwyn told me that they could. That's why I left you standing alone near the cave. I wanted to make sure I had reinforcements who could capture the monks and destroy the shrine. Fortunately, the Hammer Clan and the Painted Women had joined for another gathering in the mead hall, so I didn't need to chase after them."

"No. I meant who'd've thought that a woman left for dead only a short time ago could've made this all work."

Alerice smiled a bit sheepishly. "Oh. I've just always been a good organizer, I suppose."

Kreston turned to her, openly displaying his adoration, but she backed a half-step.

"Kreston, you should know that when this is finished, I'm going below."

"'Course, you are."

"It's not because of you."

"'Course, it's not."

"I don't know when we'll see each other again. And please don't say 'Course, you don't."

"No," he said softly.

She paused before she said, "Promise me you'll live a good life."

He nodded. She gazed up at him one final time before she turned and called to Aric. He bade her come to see what remained of the shrine, which she did.

Kreston watched her join the broad warriors. They hefted her upon their shoulders and tossed her about, which meant that more of her soul had become one with the Evherealme, a place he never wished to see again.

However, he longed to see her again. His mind began churning on some way to achieve this, but then his blood ran cold and he straightened. He was about to turn and look behind him, but *her* voice rang clearly in his mind.

"Summon your courage, Captain Dühalde," the Raven Queen said. "I wish to speak with you."

Kreston snapped to attention, 'eyes forward' as he focused on Alerice. He thought of her, and only of her. Her smile, her hair, her touch... even as the queen approached from behind and placed her willow-white hands on his shoulders.

Her touch froze him to the bone. He could only bear her presence for a few precious moments, and how he found the courage to speak to her, he had no idea. "I want to help her," he said, his voice shaking.

The Raven Queen petted the back of his salt-and-pepper head. "Because you love her."

"Yes," he gulped. "And I could be of help to her, whenever you send her back up here. If you place me in her path somehow. But... I need my mind back. She's yours, and if I'm to help her, I can't live in fear of you."

He felt the queen pet his head again, which sent shivers down his spine. No terror of a coming battle was ever as great as her dreaded caress.

"Kreston, if I unlock your mind, you will remember everything – every man you slaughtered, every task my husband forced you to undertake. I locked your thoughts away to spare you these things."

"I know." Kreston looked at Alerice, knowing something else as well. "But I need to be a whole man, White Lady. I want to be with her, even if she doesn't want to be with me."

The Raven Queen gripped Kreston's shoulders.

"So be it," she said.

Kreston felt the Raven Queen bend down and kiss the back of his head. A white light ripped across his eyes, and he saw figures come forth as though sketched in charcoal.

He saw the marshal of King Kemen of Andelous, the greedy lowlife who had betrayed the Crimson Brigade. The marshal had been Kreston's first mark, and Kreston had made his death a slow one.

Next Kreston saw the rival lords who had bribed the marshal. He saw their knights, and their squires, and so on down through the ranks. He had slaughtered them all, down to the stable hands, and from that moment he had never looked back.

After taking revenge, Kreston had done as the King of Shadows bade, moving from one battle after another, one man after another.

Kreston knew none of them. He feared none of them. His goal was to slaughter them so the King of

Shadows could claim their souls, but when he had seen that desperate captain cradling the body of his lieutenant, he saw himself cradling Landrew Mülton, the younger brother he had never had when growing up on that forsaken farm where his family had blamed him for his mother's infirmities.

That captain had not deserved to die. All the fighting men Kreston had slaughtered had not deserved to die. Their quarrel lay with their foes, not with the King of Shadows, and yet the king had claimed them, for Kreston was the enforcing agent sent to butcher them.

Then in a terrible moment of recollection, Kreston saw the face of the runner boy he had stalked. Next, he saw the faces of the other boys, helpless children who could never have outfought him even if he hadn't wielded the king's broadsword.

Then he saw the nurses. He remembered how they had huddled together, bravely praying to the Raven Queen even though they knew their fate was sealed.

How could he have done all this? Had he ever attempted to deny the King of Shadows and rebel against his orders? Yes. He had, but only once, for the king had tormented him with the Crimson Brigade's loss over and over until he had capitulated.

Kreston had learned to summon ice into his veins long ago, but the ice the King of Shadows inspired had made Kreston more obdurate than the world's hardest stone.

Now he was no longer. Kreston fell to his knees on

the plateau and held his hands out above his head, palms up as he begged, "White Lady! Let me atone. Show me how I may be forgiven. Show me how I may tip the balance of my defaults so that when you measure me, you may find at least one merit by which I may redeem myself. Please, White Lady. Help me!"

"There is no help for you, Dühalde," a dark voice said.

Kreston's heart seized. He felt a veil wrap tightly around him, just as it had when the King of Shadows had held him captive in the Realme's landscape of glowing blooms. The king had forced him to stand in a suspended state while Alerice conversed with him, and now that same state enveloped him and held him steady, his palms still high overhead.

"There is no atonement," the King of Shadows said. "You should resign yourself to doing what you do best, and for that you will need this."

Kreston managed to look up at the dreaded shade looming over him. The King of Shadows drew his Realme broadsword and placed the handle in Kreston's right hand.

Kreston could not stop his fingers from closing around it. He could not stop his hand from gripping it tightly. He could not move as the King of Shadows stepped in, reached to his forehead, and raked his iron fingernails across his brow.

Kreston tried to strangle a cry as the king again branded him with a mark of wide striations. He felt the Realme claim him once again. He felt his soul tethered and bound, and though he had vowed to fight the King of Shadows should he try to recapture him, Kreston was powerless to prevent his return to bondage.

Just as he had told Alerice when encouraging her to run after the Raven Queen had released her, once the Realme had him, it could always take him back.

"And welcome back," the King of Shadows said. "And welcome back to your mind. I knew if I freed you, you would find some way to pledge yourself to the girl so convincingly that my wife would free you. And you did. And it worked. But you are mine, Dühalde. You will be until the day I let you die. Now, you are ready to kill again in my name? Let's see what the girl thinks of you once she watches you do what you have always done best."

"I already know what I think of him, Your Majesty," Kreston heard Alerice say. He tried to find her, to gaze upon her, but she stood somewhere behind the King of Shadows, and he could not see her. Nor could he call out to her. He could do nothing to protect her.

To Alerice, this moment was sadly predictable. She stood, arms folded, behind the King of Shadows. She could not see Kreston, for the king had veiled him. She had been looking directly at Kreston before the king had made him disappear. Then the king had engaged in conversation, which meant that Kreston was still at hand, hidden and likely in a dire situation.

"Let him go, Your Majesty," Alerice calmly asserted.

The King of Shadows turned about to gaze down on her. He pressed his dark gray eyes into hers, but they did not affect her. He stepped forward to tower over her, but he inspired no fear. She was more than the Raven Queen's Walker now. She bore the mark of Imari and the kiss of Sukaar. She had won the alliance of the Hammer Clan, the Painted Women, and the Wyld. And she was going to help Kreston Dühalde.

"Never order me, girl," the King of Shadows said.

"Then please let me see him, Your Majesty," Alerice offered.

The king took one more step to close the distance, and Alerice arched her back and raised her head.

Locking stares with the king, she stated, "You will not dare strike at me, Your Majesty. For in so doing, you will be declaring war upon your wife. Is that what you truly wish? War within the Realme? Your wife does not wish that. Imari and Sukaar do not wish that. You have no power over me, and I implore you, with all respect. Let me see Kreston Dühalde."

The King of Shadows narrowed his dark gray gaze, but he lifted an arm so that the crystalline trim on the sleeves of his long robe caught the moonlight. Then he banished the veil, and Kreston to fell forward.

Alerice wanted to bolt for him and lift him

into her arms, but she forced herself to take a measured breath and remain in locked stares with the Evherealme's master.

"Thank you, Your Majesty."

Alerice paced past the King of Shadows, shocked at her own deliberately even steps. Had this been the very shade she had met in the Hall of Eternity not so very long ago? Had he been the same immortal who had inspired her to dread herself? Perhaps, but no longer.

She crossed to Kreston, and extended her hand. He grasped her forearm, and she pulled him to his feet. She regarded him, and then regarded the broadsword set in his hand. She saw his hazel eyes begging her to leave him to his fate, but she was not about to do anything of the sort.

Alerice turned about to face the king, planting herself between Kreston and his vilified master.

"You are about to send Kreston back into battle to harvest souls for you. You will no doubt prevent the queen from locking his mind away again, and you have no care if Kreston loses it in forced servitude to you.

"But you have overlooked one last move in this game: mine. Kreston may slay men in your name. He may again become the Ghost of the Crimson Brigade, but I will be there to make certain he never goes too far. I will be his advocate against you. So as I told you earlier, two Walkers now stand before you, and neither of us will be of much use to you."

The King of Shadows looked Alerice over. "I told you that you are better than he is. Enjoy your self-assuredness, Alerice Linden of Navre. You're going to need it."

The King of Shadows waved his arm once again, and both he and Kreston vanished from the plateau.

Tales of the Ravensdaughter
will continue with
Adventure Six
The Raven's Daughter

PLEASE REVIEW THIS BOOK:

If you enjoyed *Mistress of Her Own Game*, please leave a review.

AMAZON

GOODREADS

AUTHOR'S WEBSITE

Thank you and blessings,
Erin Hunt Rado
ErinRadoAuthor.com

BOOKS IN THIS SERIES

Tales of the Ravensdaughter
- Collection One

The Beast Of Basque

The Thief Of Souls

The Wizard And The Wyld

Rips In The Ether

Mistress Of Her Own Game

The Raven's Daughter

Made in the USA
Columbia, SC
19 October 2022

69674380R10050